INVASION OF THE BLACK GEARS

DIGITAL DIGIMON MONSTERS

A. RYAN NERZ

HarperEntertainment
An Imprint of HarperCollinsPublishers

📽 HarperEntertainment

An Imprint of HarperCollins*Publishers*

10 East 53rd Street, New York, NY 10022-5299

ISBN 0-06-107187-0

First printing: June 2000

Printed in the United States of America

Visit HarperEntertainment on the World Wide Web at www.harpercollins.com

❖ 10 9 8 7 6 5 4 3 2 1

1

Their adventure begins. . . .

One moment, they were at summer camp. Tai was lounging up in a tree, catching some rays. Sora and Mimi were chatting about the things they missed back home. Matt was playing the harmonica while his little brother, T.K., listened. Izzy was typing on his laptop computer, and Joe was complaining about his allergies.

Suddenly, the clouds turned black, and it started snowing like crazy . . . a blizzard in the middle of the summer! And all seven kids felt themselves rise into the air and, for a brief moment, totally *disappear*.

When the crew finally rematerialized, they found

themselves on a strange island. A *digital* island, full of digital monsters, Digimons. In fact, each kid found his own personal Digimon friend waiting there. Which was a good thing. Because with all the adventures that lay ahead, they would need all the friends they could get. . . .

"Yo, Agumon," Tai shouted out to his new buddy.

"What's up, Tai?" Agumon asked.

"I liked it when you digivolved into Greymon and kicked Shellmon's butt!" Tai said. "Why don't you just stay Greymon all the time?"

"I'd love to," Agumon shot back. "But I can't. Even heroes need a rest."

Just then, totally out of nowhere, came the loudest, scariest growl they had ever heard. It was so loud that the ground started to tremble. Tai nearly fell backward over a cliff.

"ARRRRRRRR!"

"What's that noise?" Tai asked. "Whoa!"

The entire gang looked up at once. And there it was. A triceratops! Okay, it wasn't

really a dinosaur, but it looked like one. That's because it was a Dinosaur Digimon named Monochromon, a huge gray monster with a giant tusk, scaly back, and a whiplike tail. He didn't seem to be in a very good mood.

"ARRRRRRRR!"

"Oh, no!" Joe said. His eyes were about to pop out of his head. "There are two of them!"

On the other side of the gang was another Monochromon, gnashing its teeth angrily. Both of them looked like they hadn't eaten yet. In a situation like that, there's really just one option.

"Let's run!" Tai shouted. Joe and Sora didn't even hear him. They were already sprinting away at full speed, and the entire gang wasn't far behind.

They ducked on the far side of some big rocks, just out of sight.

CRASH!

Tai looked from behind the rocks toward the crash. The Monochromons had head-butted each other. One of them whipped its huge tail around, and a rock the size of a boulder flew through the air. The Monochromons didn't even seem to notice that the crew had run away. They almost looked like they were fighting . . . each other.

"Something must've set those Monochromons off," Tai said.

"They're fighting over territory!" Tentomon shouted.

"*ROWRRR!*" the Monochromon roared.

Mimi saw her Digimon's flowery head sprint away. "Hey, Palmon!" she yelled at the top of her lungs. "Don't leave without me!" Mimi started running, and Sora, Izzy, and Joe followed.

"They definitely don't need us hanging

around," Tai agreed, accelerating to top speed. They were all running so fast. That is, except T.K., whose little legs couldn't keep up the pace. The harder he tried, the more T.K. fell behind, until he tripped on a rock and hit the dirt.

"T.K.!" Matt said, stopping in his tracks. As much as Matt tries to act cool, he always looks out for his little brother.

Another loud crash came from the direction of the Monochromons. Matt reached out his hand to help T.K. to his feet.

Tai looked back over his shoulder and noticed they were in danger. "Hurry up, you guys!"

"We're coming!" T.K. yelled back, trying to sound as in control as possible. Before Matt could help him, T.K. was up and running.

But just as T.K. and Matt caught up to the gang, they heard the crunch of the Monochromons locking horns. And then a loud grinding sound. And then . . . SPLASH! The Monochromons glided off a cliff together and landed in the river.

The kids were safe—for the time being.

2

Whew!

That seems to be a common reaction in DigiWorld. And that's how the whole crew felt after their meeting with the Monochromons. *Relieved.* Well, except for Mimi.

"I don't walk this much unless I'm at a mall," Mimi whined. She leaned against a big tree. "And as you can see, we're nowhere near one."

Agumon walked up behind Mimi and tried to console her. "Maybe if you take off your boots and socks, you'd feel better," he said.

Mimi turned around and looked at Agumon like he was a monster. (Oh, yeah. He actually *is* a

monster.) "I'm *not* walking on dirt in my bare feet!" Mimi said. (If her fashionable cowboy hat didn't tip you off, Mimi's a real girly girl.)

Palmon walked over and flashed a huge smile. "I love the feel of dirt under my feet, especially between my toes!"

"Gross!" Mimi said.

Izzy scratched his head. "It appears that we might be losing our light source."

Sora stared off into the horizon. "And that sunset looks weird."

"This whole island's weird!" Izzy added. "We need to find a place to hide. . . . Who knows what will come out at night?"

All of a sudden, Izzy's Digimon, Tentomon, flew off into the air. "Wait, I detect water!" he called out. "As usual, I'm right! It's a lake with fresh, clean water and a variety of tasty fish!"

"Yeah! We get to swim!" Gomamon yelled out. He's a Sea Animal Digimon who's

 friends with all the fish.

Gomamon charged for the water, but–*splat!*–fell right on his face. Somebody had grabbed his tail.

"Gomamon!" Joe said to his Digimon friend. "You better wait and make sure it's safe first!"

"Everybody's hungry. We have to find some food," Tai said. He thinks he's the leader of the group.

They walked. Then they walked some more. Finally, they came to an enormous pink lake. That's right, a *pink* lake. And in the distance, rising above the other side of the lake, were blue mountains.

This DigiWorld place was getting weirder by the second.

The gang stopped at the shore.

"It should be safe to rest here tonight," said Biyomon.

"Yeah, I love camping outside," Sora stated.

Mimi stared at Sora, alarmed. "If I don't walk on dirt, what makes you think I'll sleep in it!"

"Mimi, do you see a hotel here?" Tai asked.

"Whoa!" Mimi gasped, pointing at something behind Tai.

The gang looked toward a bright light sparking and twinkling in the distance. It appeared to be coming from something sitting right in the middle of the lake.

"It looks like a trolley car," T.K. said matter-of-factly.

"The lights just came on!" Izzy added.

"Maybe there are some real people in there," Sora said.

Tai didn't hesitate for a second. "Let's check it out!" he yelled, already running toward it.

As it turned out, the trolley car was on an island with a narrow path of land leading to it. The kids raced over as fast as they could, their hopes already getting the best of them.

"Maybe they can take us back home . . . in air-conditioned comfort!" Mimi said, running ahead of everyone else.

By the time Tai arrived, Mimi was already sitting on one of the trolley seats, smiling. But there was no one else in sight.

"Bummer," Tai said. "It's empty!"

"No trolley car is this clean!" Izzy added. "We must be its first passengers. . . ."

"Oh, goody," Mimi said, nestling into the clean vinyl seats. "These cushions are comfy."

Tai scratched his head. "Something's not right here."

"At least it's cozy. I say we stay," Sora said.

"Ohhh, can we eat now?" Tentomon asked, holding his stomach.

3

The whole gang went off to round up food. That is, except for Gomamon.

He went to swim and splash around in the lake.

"Gomamon!" Izzy yelled, while fishing on the lakeshore. "Stop playing in the water. I can't catch any fish if you keep warning them away."

Meanwhile, Tentomon had flown up to a tree to stuff his face with natural foods. "Yum, yum!" he said, chomping away. "You can't get too many berries down the hatch."

Patamon used his Boom Bubble

to huff and puff and . . . knock a batch of bananas out of a tree.

Even Mimi was trying to help gather food. She found a big batch of mushrooms at the base of a tree.

Palmon walked up to her. "Those are bad mushrooms. You shouldn't pick 'em—they'll make you sick!"

Mimi gasped. "I'd be a big mess without you, Palmon. You're the best!"

Matt, Sora, and Tai gathered sticks for a fire and piled them up by the riverbank.

"We're all set to cook dinner," Matt said. "Now all we need is the grub!"

"That would be great," Sora said, throwing her hands in the air. "But how are we supposed to light the fire?"

"Like this!" Agumon exclaimed. He instantly ignited the fire with his flaming Pepper Breath. "How's that for teamwork!"

"Yeah, Agumon," Tai said. "You're the man!"

Izzy arrived with his arms full. "We caught a bunch of fish!"

"Awesome job, Izzy!" Tai said. "Let's eat."

After the fish were cooked, the whole crew happily munched away.

"This is surprisingly good," remarked Biyomon.

"Matt, Mom only lets me eat fish sticks," T.K. said.

"Mom's not around now," Matt said, a lit-

tle annoyed. "So just eat."

"Okay," T.K. said. He sank his teeth into the fish he held.

After they finished their meal, Tai approached Sora, who sat by the riverbank.

"Matt doesn't treat T.K. like a brother, only like he's a *bother*," Tai said. "Is it just me, or have you noticed that, too?"

"Yeah," Sora agreed. "It's just that Matt's still learning how to be a big brother."

Tai nodded. "Maybe you're right."

Joe joined them. He looked up into the sky and sighed.

"Whatcha lookin' at?" Sora asked him.

"I'm trying to find out which direction we've been going," Joe said. "But I can't find the North Star anywhere."

"You're right!" Sora said. "I don't recognize any of these constellations either."

"You're forgetting your astronomy," Tai said. "If you can't see the North Star, then

it must be on the other side of the world."

Sora looked at Tai, concerned. "Do you think we could be in the southern hemisphere?"

"I guess it's possible," Joe answered. "That is, if we're still on Earth."

They heard a loud yawn behind them. It was Patamon.

"Look," T.K. said. "They're getting tired!"

The Digimons were beyond tired. Palmon and Gomamon were already snoring, and Patamon passed out immediately after yawning.

"I'm getting really tired myself," Tai said.

"Wait a second, before everyone falls asleep," Izzy said. "I think we all need to take turns standing guard."

"How about each of us stands guard for an hour," Tai said.

"Not T.K.," Matt said. He can be so protective of his little brother sometimes.

"C'mon, Matt!" T.K. urged. "Tai said I'm a big boy now!"

"No," Matt said in his most fatherly tone. "You're too young, and you need your rest."

"I'm getting cold," Mimi said. "I need a warm blanket to help me sleep."

"Hey, Gabumon!" Tai exclaimed. "Watch it! Mimi may sneak up on you and steal your fur!"

Tai smiled and grabbed Gabumon's tail, teasing him.

"Stop it, Tai." Gabumon scampered away. "That's not funny!"

Matt pushed Tai back. "Yeah, quit it!"

"What are you buggin' about?" Tai asked.

Matt's jaw was suddenly tight. "Gabumon told you to stop! So, knock it off!"

"Hey!" Tai said. "You can't tell me what to do!"

Matt and Tai grabbed each other's shirts, then started pushing. Tai pulled his fists back, ready to fight.

"Stop fighting!" T.K. yelled. Matt and Tai let go at the same time. They turned their backs on one another and folded their arms.

"You'd both make great guards," Joe said. "Who wants to go first?"

"I will!" Tai said.

"I'm next!" Matt chimed in.

"Good," Joe said. "I propose that we all trek back to the trolley car and get some shut-eye."

Tai stood guard while the rest of the crew returned to the bus and settled in for a long night's rest—or so they hoped. . . .

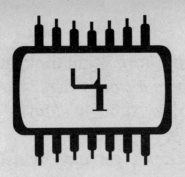

4

The kids and their Digimons were per-
fectly snuggled for sleep inside the trolley
car. While the Digimons huddled on the
floor, the kids stretched out on the trolley
seats. Perfect sleeping accommodations . . .
almost.

"G'night," Joe said.

"Don't let the Monochromons bite!" T.K.
added, grinning.

*Thanks for reminding me about the
Monochromons, T.K.,* Sora thought.

My feet still hurt, Mimi thought.

Why is there a trolley here? . . . Maybe it's the aliens, Izzy thought. *Maybe they knew we needed it. . . .*

I hope I don't get any monster cooties! thought Joe.

Matt was the only one who couldn't sleep. He was snuggled up beside Gabumon with his eyes wide open.

"Gabumon," Matt said.

"Yeah?" Gabumon replied.

"Go over and lay down with my brother. . . ."

"Why, Matt?" Gabumon asked.

"Because your fur's makin' me sweat!" Matt barked. "Now, go!"

"Because you want me to keep T.K. warm," Gabumon said.

"Hey," Matt shot back. "I didn't say that!"

"You just don't want to admit it," Gabumon said.

"Whatever!" Matt said.

Gabumon snuggled next to T.K. on the trolley seat. T.K. felt the warmth and awakened. He saw Gabumon, then noticed his brother, Matt, staring at him with a concerned look on his face.

"Ahhh!" T.K. said. "Thanks, Matt!"

Matt blushed and turned away. He still couldn't sleep, so he walked out of the trolley into the night.

Meanwhile, Tai and Agumon were sitting by the fire, keeping watch. But Tai was so exhausted that he kept nodding off.

"Tai, don't fall asleep on your first night-watch!" Agumon said.

Tai stood up and yawned. "My eyes won't stay open. I'll go to the lake and splash some water on my face to wake up."

Tai heard a noise behind him as he bent down to the water. "Who's there?" he asked. He turned his head and saw . . . Matt standing behind him.

"What, you don't think I can handle the lookout by myself?" Tai asked.

"No, I couldn't sleep," Matt answered.

"Oh, yeah? And why's that?" Tai asked.

"Look, I'm sorry about earlier," Matt said. "I didn't mean to fly off the handle, it's just that being here, and having to watch T.K. . . ."

"Do you guys even live in the same house?" Tai asked.

"Not anymore," Matt replied. "We're half brothers, and we don't get to see each other that much."

"Well, that explains a lot," Tai said.

Matt grunted and ran away.

Moments later, a beautiful, melodious sound swept over the lake.

"What a wonderful sound," Gabumon said to Matt, who held a harmonica in his hands.

"Yeah, wonderful," Tai said, a little jealous. "Maybe to a Saint Bernard with a horn on his forehead."

The beautiful harmonica music filled the air, but peace rarely lasts long in DigiWorld. Over the harmonica, a faint rumbling could be heard. The ground began to shake. Then, as if that weren't enough, the lake began to swell and swirl into big waves. Tidal waves!

Matt jumped, tossing his harmonica. "Oh, no!"

"*Ahhhh!*" Tai and Agumon screamed in unison.

In a flash, the surface of the water burst, and something pushed its way upward with a deafening roar. It thrust higher and higher into the sky, growling and twisting. It was huge. And green. And extremely angry.

It was a sea monster!

5

"What's that horrible sound?" Sora asked from inside the trolley.

"It's an earthquake!" Mimi shouted.

"The trolley's starting to move!" Joe yelled. "And I don't think it's taking us home!"

"It's taking us toward that sea dragon!" Izzy said.

"Oh, no!" Tentomon shrieked. "Seadramon!"

The kids saw, from the windows of the trol-

ley, the most enormous sea serpent they could possibly imagine. It was so big that the land that the trolley car was on was resting on its back! With each growl, its enormous teeth gnashed, and its head whipped furiously from side to side.

"We're gonna get eaten for sure!" Mimi cried.

Seadramon began to charge through the water.

"Hold on!" Agumon screamed.

"It's like we're on a monster-long board," Tai said.

"He's pulling us along by his tail," Izzy said. "I don't even think he realizes we're here."

"Perhaps not, he's a bit dense. As long as

he doesn't see us, we're okay," said Tentomon as he stopped onto a red patch on the ground.

"Don't be too sure!" Agumon said.

With a loud snap, Seadramon's tail whipped toward them and knocked Tentomon out into the lake.

"I guess he does know we're here," said Izzy.

"Aahh!" Tai said. "That big red thing was his tail!"

Seadramon's tail whipped across again, and knocked them all backward. The land wasn't attached to his tail anymore, but Seadramon was still mad! He swam beneath the island and pushed it, racing full-speed toward the shore.

"We're gonna crash into the shore!" Joe said.

Matt watched in horror from the other shore where he'd run to play his harmonica before it all began.

Matt jumped into the water to save his little brother. "T.K.!"

Gabumon followed Matt to the edge of the water. "Matt, I'm just letting you know my fur's gonna get wet, and I'm gonna stink!" Gabumon leaped into the water and followed Matt, who was swimming with all his strength to save T.K.

Seadramon suddenly stopped and remained silent for a few seconds.

"Great!" Tai shouted. "He left us right in the middle of the lake!"

"I don't suppose we could trick him into taking us back," Izzy said.

Seadramon's serpent head burst through the water with a loud growl.

"*ROWRRRRR!*"

"Get ready!" Tai said. "He's attacking!"

"Come on, guys!" Agumon said. "Let's send him back to the fishies!"

"No problem!" Gabumon shouted.

"SPIRAL TWISTER!" Biyomon said, shooting her spiraling attack, which bounced right off Seadramon's neck.

Patamon launched a speedy ball from her mouth. "BOOM BUBBLE!" But Seadramon didn't even seem to notice.

"POISON IVY!" Palmon yelled, shooting

green stems into the air. They fell short before reaching Seadramon.

Tentomon flew upward, right into Seadramon's face. "SUPER SHOCKER!" he shouted, shooting off his lightning rod attack.

"PEPPER BREATH!" Agumon shot his fireball upward. It hit Seadramon in the face, but the serpent didn't even flinch.

"Agumon!" Tai shouted. "Digivolve!"

"I've been trying," Agumon said. "But I can't seem to do it this time, Tai."

Tai flashed him a hopeless look. "You have to!"

Agumon shrugged. "Maybe my body hasn't recovered from that fight with Shellmon."

"But if you can't help us, how are we going to stop Seadramon?" Tai shouted.

"T.K.! Over here!"

The voice came from the water. Matt was still swimming toward them!

"Matt, be careful! Or

the monster will get you!" T.K. said. Just as the last word left T.K.'s mouth, Seadramon shook the ground, and T.K. and Gomamon fell into the water. Luckily, Gomamon kept T.K.'s head above water.

"Gomamon, go!" Joe cheered.

"ROWWRRR!"

"Get out fast!" Tentomon warned. "It's Seadramon! He's back!"

"Gomamon," Matt said. "You can do it!"

"Right!" Gomamon agreed, and swam T.K. toward the shore.

Worried that Seadramon might attack his little brother, Matt decided to play decoy.

He swam toward the middle of the lake, in plain sight. "Hey," Matt taunted. "Over here, you overgrown water-lizard!"

Gabumon followed Matt to keep him out of danger.

"BLUE BLASTER! Haaaa!" Gabumon yelled. He spit a ball of blazing blue fire at Seadramon.

But Seadramon fended off the attack and, with a quick flip of his tail, sent Gabumon

flying through the air into the distance.

"I-I-I-I hate this!" Gabumon shrieked.

Just then Seadramon grabbed Matt and dragged him deep under the water.

"Matt was only trying to save me!" T.K. said. "It's all my fault. . . . I'll never forgive myself!"

Just as the words fell from T.K.'s mouth, he heard his brother's wild scream. Seadramon pulled Matt out of the water.

"Oh, no!" Tai said.

"This isn't good!" said Tentomon. "Seadramon may be a bubble brain, but once he finds his prey, he won't let go!"

"Matt," T.K. screamed at his brother. "Hang on!"

Matt groaned loudly, trying to free himself. Or at least, trying to breathe.

"Patamon! Please help him!" T.K. pleaded.

"Hit him with a Boom Bubble!"

Patamon shook his head helplessly. "Seadramon's too big. I don't have enough power now. . . . Gabumon, you're stronger. What can you do?"

"You're right. Matt is in trouble and I must help him," Gabumon said bravely.

"GABUMON!" Matt screamed at the top of his lungs.

"Don't give up!" T.K. yelled to his brother. "I'll find a way to save you, if it's the last thing I do!"

"Matt, hold on!" Gabumon added.

"GABUMON!" Matt pleaded again.

Gabumon said the magic words: "Gabumon, digivolve into Garurumon!"

A beam of light shot from the digivice on Matt's waist toward Gabumon. Gabumon flashed bright silver, then was surrounded by a swirl of lightning flashes. He spun around several times, and then disappeared, and then . . .

GARURUMON!

Gabumon had transformed into an enormous white-and-blue arctic wolf-looking beast. Garurumon. He had immense dagger-like teeth and giant paws with tremendous blood-red claws. Whew!

Garurumon took four giant strides and leaped at Seadramon in the water. He bit into Seadramon's tail with his teeth, and the sea monster's grip on Matt was instantly released. Matt fell on the ground next to his brother with a thud.

"Are you all right, Matt?" T.K. asked.

"Yeah," Matt responded, shaking off the fall. "But where's Gabumon?"

Seadramon had forced Garurumon into the water, where Seadramon had the advantage.

But Garurumon held his own. He skimmed the top of the water almost like a dolphin, dodging Seadramon's blows.

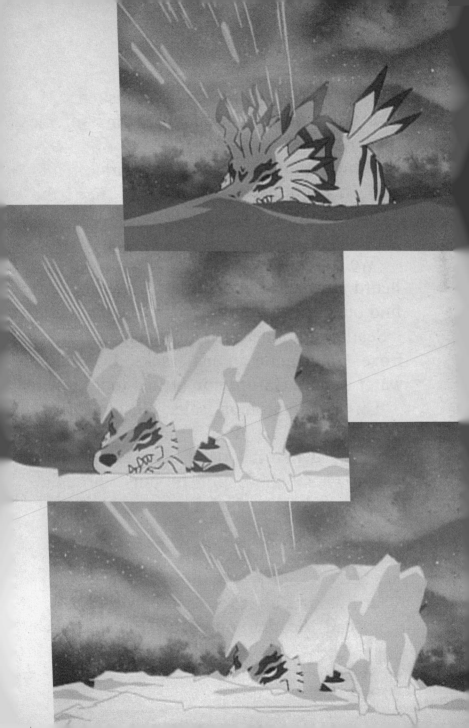

"Garurumon's fur is legendary," Tentomon said. "He's like a growling steel torpedo."

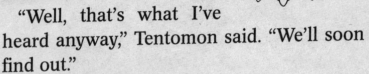

"That's astonishing," Izzy shot back. "Then he must be invincible."

"Well, that's what I've heard anyway," Tentomon said. "We'll soon find out."

Seadramon unleashed an icy blue ray that froze Garurumon in his tracks. Even the water around Garurumon turned to ice!

"Uh-oh!" Tentomon said. "Seadramon's using his lethal Ice Blast!"

But just when it looked like Garurumon was down for the count, he burst through the ice and unleashed his own blue ray attack.

"HOWLING BLASTER!" Garurumon shrieked.

Garurumon's attack was so powerful that it pushed Seadramon's Ice Blast back toward him for an extra knockout punch. The combined force knocked Seadramon backward into the water, causing a gargantuan splash!

T.K. and Matt put their hands up in victory. "Hooray!" they yelled.

Seadramon was defeated. Garurumon returned to his Gabumon level. He came ashore, looking exhausted . . . and small.

Matt happily greeted him. "Gabumon!"

"Flying sure is a good way to keep my fur dry," Gabumon said.

"You digivolved into Garurumon just in

time," Matt said proudly.

T.K. gave Gabumon a big hug. "Oh, Gabumon! Thanks for saving my brother."

"Anytime, little friend," said Gabumon warmly.

"Matt, you were so awesome against that nasty monster," T.K. said.

"You think so?" Matt asked nonchalantly.

"You know you were the man!" Gabumon said.

Matt looked at him. "And you're the *wolf* man!"

Matt and T.K. laughed, and soon the others were all holding their bellies. When you survive a battle with a huge sea serpent, laughter is *really* a relief.

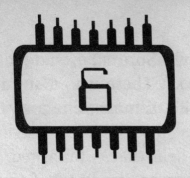

Another exciting adventure behind them, Matt, Tai, Sora, and the rest of the crew did the only thing that made any sense. They walked. And walked. Away from Seadramon's lake and deep into the forest. They were searching for some clue, maybe another human to talk to, anything. . . .

There had to be a way out of this freaky digitized world filled with overgrown sea serpents, tidal waves, cliffs, random road signs, and monsters of all shapes and sizes. There had to be a way back home to malls, summer camp, pizza parties, and ice cream. *Home.* Where the scariest creatures around were the monsters from video games. Now it seemed like they were stuck *inside* a video game. Would they ever escape?

"Heyyyyy!" Sora said, suddenly stopping in her tracks. There was a strange buzzing sound in the distance, like a swarm of wild bees.

"Do you hear that?" Tai asked.

"It seems to be some sort of aircraft," Matt answered.

They hurried to the edge of the forest just in time to see a big blur fly into the trees.

"It looked like a big flying gear," Sora said.

"Admit it," Izzy said, raising his finger to make his point. "My alien theory is becoming more plausible."

T.K. leaned forward to get a look at the

giant flying object. He slipped and almost fell down a steep hill.

"T.K.!" Sora said. Tai grabbed T.K. by the shoulder and pulled him back.

"That was scary!" T.K. whimpered in reply.

"Watch it," Matt said.

"That coulda been a snake," Tai cried. "Or worse!"

"Gee, I'm sorry," T.K. said. "Hey, Biyomon. Are there really snakes here?"

Biyomon smiled. "No, just giant flying

killer bugs and other unpleasant Digimons."

"Don't worry, T.K." Patamon fluttered his wings. "I'll take care of them!" Patamon flew into T.K.'s arms and giggled.

Sora put her hands on her hips. "Okay, now that that's settled, let's get going."

"Yeah, this is dumb," Tai huffed. "I say we keep moving and see if we can find any signs of intelligent life."

"Wait a minute," Biyomon protested. "Is he saying that we Digimons are not intelligent? Is that what he's saying?"

"Not at all," Sora said reassuringly. "But I think Tai is right. We need to keep moving in hopes of finding out where we are." Sora closed her eyes and tried to think of a way to  cheer up the others. "We need to stay calm and stick together. Let's remember, we're in this together . . ."

"Together sounds good!" cried Biyomon.

"Moving right along, folks," Matt joked as they walked. "Keep it moving. Our next stop on the tour will be the forest of irrelevant road signs. No pictures, please."

Sora looked noticeably irritatied. *We're lost in the middle of nowhere, and these guys are making jokes,* she thought.

"Look!" Matt exclaimed, walking in front as usual. "Telephone poles! I say we follow them and see where they lead."

"They'll just lead to trouble," Joe groaned.

Just up ahead, beyond a clearing in the forest, was a vast desert filled with telephone poles. There must have been thousands of them, all leaning to the side as if they hadn't been used in years. How could that be explained? Not that anything else in DigiWorld made much sense. So the gang walked toward them into the hot, dry desert air.

"Boy, it's so hot I can feel the heat coming up through my socks," T.K. said, already starting to sweat.

"Maybe you should put your shoes back on," Matt said.

"This hot desert air is destroying my complexion!" Mimi exclaimed. "How much farther is it?"

"Hey!" Sora said, changing the subject suddenly. "Does anybody besides me see that these telephone poles have no connecting wires?"

"She's right," agreed Izzy. "I wonder if these actually *are* telephone poles. Maybe they're some odd alien equivalent."

Mimi looked at her wrist, confused. "You won't believe what happened to my favorite

watch. The sun melted the numbers right off!" Mimi almost shouted. They all looked at her watch.

"Mimi, that's not a watch. It's a compass!" said Izzy. "For someone who hates hiking, you sure have a lot of compasses," Izzy continued. The compass needle then started spinning wildly out of control.

"Huhhh?" Joe remarked, his eyes wide with amazement.

"Of course," Izzy said to Mimi. "None of your compasses actually work."

Izzy's gaze turned from the compass to the sand beneath his feet. His brain started churning. He bent down and ran a small pile of sand through his fingers. "The dirt contains small traces of metal, which can

affect the compass needle," Izzy observed.

Mimi shrugged. "Oh well, I'm always late anyway."

Sora stood up and put her hands on her hips. "This is one weird world and I don't like it one little bit!" she said.

"I think we should start looking for water, guys," Izzy said. "Otherwise, we could dehydrate in all this heat."

Mimi arched her back and looked up to the sky. She couldn't take it anymore. The heat. The telephone poles with no tele-

phones. The crazy compass. The lack of designer shoes.

"Hellllp!" Mimi shouted desperately into the desert air. "Somebody please find us!"

7

"Hang on just a little longer." Tai remained positive, regardless of how much trouble they were in. "Don't give up now!"

Palmon looked really scorched. She slumped over. "My head is baking," she said. "If this goes on too much longer, I'm going to look like a wilted salad."

"We're gonna be okay," Mimi said, concerned. "Just keep movin' along." She took off her cowboy hat and turned to Palmon. "Here, you wear my hat for a while. You need it more than I do."

"Thank you, Mimi," Palmon said.

"*Pyewww*," T.K. said, sniffing the air. "What's that smell?"

"Now you know why they call

 57

them *sweat* socks," Matt quipped.

"This beach would be a lot more popular if it just had a couple more things," Mimi said, trying to keep the conversation light. "Like an ocean, a gentle breeze, a snack bar, hunky lifeguards . . ." Mimi giggled.

"Wait," Tai interrupted. "Hold on just a second, everybody. If I'm seeing what I *think* I'm seeing."

"What is it, Tai?" T.K. asked.

Tai pulled out his binoculars to get a better look. "It's not a mirage. . . ." he said. "It's *real water*!"

"Water?!" Sora and Biyomon yelled it at the same time.

"This is fantastic!" Joe said, perking up. "Now all we need are lemons, sugar, and some big fat ice cubes."

Izzy's eyes grew big. "That looks like a village. Maybe we'll find people!"

"And shade!" Palmon added.

"Maybe they'll have hats for sale," Mimi said. "Hang on!"

"Great!" Tai shouted. "Let's get off this desert!"

"Yayyyy!" Sora cheered.

"Hooraayyy!" Matt chipped in.

And even though the sun had totally drained their energy, the kids and their Digimons ran as fast as they could toward the village in the distance.

As the kids ran toward the village, they had no idea of the evil lurking in their midst. A black disk flew out of the side of a mountain, spiraling through the air at great speed. It sailed downward toward the Digimon that guards Mount Miharashi, and lodged itself deep in his stomach. This Digimon, who under normal circumstances was fairly good-hearted, was now under the evil rule of the Black Gear. And the kids would feel its wrath soon enough. . . .

But the kids and their Digimons couldn't have been less concerned. As they approached the little village, they heard a volley of high-pitched cheers and greetings.

"Ahhhh!"

"Ohhhh!"

"Eeeee!"

They were suddenly surrounded by hundreds of little Digimons. They looked like pink flowers with green eyes and blue petals sprouting from their heads. Their little gray huts were sprinkled everywhere like mushrooms. The little Digimons were called Yokomons, and they weren't even tall enough to reach Matt's knees.

"From the distance everything looked so big," Tai said.

"But they're so cute and tiny," Mimi countered.

Biyomon didn't waste any time. She cut straight to the important stuff. "Okay, who here knows where we can get a drink?" she asked.

"And just what do giant Digimons drink?" one of the Yokomons asked.

"Me?" Sora said. "I'm no Digimon."

"My friend Sora is what's called a human being," Biyomon explained. "Yes, we know they look funny. In spite of this, they are all actually very nice."

"What's a human being?" two Yokomons asked at once.

Another Yokomon jumped up and down with excitement. "If you are not a Digimon, what are you doing here in DigiWorld?"

Before the crew could answer, the Yokomons began shooting questions and

"Those Monochromons definitely don't need us hanging around!"

Matt and Tai get hot under the collar . . .

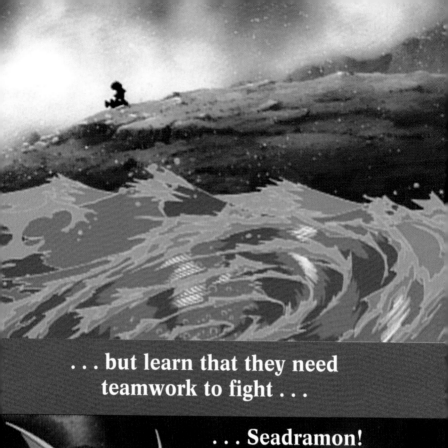

. . . but learn that they need
teamwork to fight . . .

. . . Seadramon!

Garurumon unleashes his mighty Howling Blaster!

Invasion of the Black Gear!

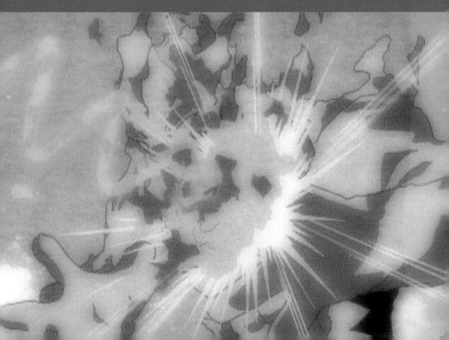

"Go away, Meramon! We're not bothering you!"

Meramon feels the sting of Birdramon's fierce Meteor Wing Attack.

"I'll remember
this day forever, Sora."

comments at the gang, rapid-fire.

"Oh, my," Mimi said. "I would love to just take one home and put her on my bed with all my other stuffed animals."

Patamon looked at his human friend and shook his head. "T.K. is very, very tired," he said. "And even more—very, very hungry."

"He's not the only one," Joe chimed in.

"Biyomon," one of the Yokomons asked. "Just when did you digivolve from a Yokomon?"

"When I met Sora," Biyomon answered

with a smile. "We share a special bond which is magical."

"You don't talk like us anymore," the Yokomon stated. "Is that how all Biyomons talk?"

"No, it's how the big ones talk." Biyomon shrugged. "I suppose I just picked it up from Sora. She is a wonderful and kind human being and I've already learned a lot from her."

Another Yokomon stepped up. "We still don't understand how you digivolved. What is it about being around human beings that makes it happen?"

"Sora needed me," Biyomon explained. "And I had to protect her. When she was in danger, a power came flowing through me. . . ."

Sora sat by herself to think it through. *She* had to protect *me*? she asked herself. *Wait a second, now I get it. That's why she's been following me around.* Sora put her head in her hands and thought back to when the other Digimons had digivolved. Aloud, she realized, "When Tai needed him, Agumon digivolved into Greymon to protect him. And Gabumon did the same for Matt. They digivolved for us!" Sora's face widened with a big smile as she thought back on the times their Digimon friends had saved them from danger. "We're lucky kids!" she concluded.

"Sora!" Biyomon said, interrupting her human friend. "We're invited to have dinner with the Yokos. They said they'd be willing to share their food with all of us."

"Oh, wow!" Sora beamed.

"Yayyy!" the whole gang cheered.

"Let's see hands if you want lemonade!" Joe shouted.

"I'll take a cheeseburger, fries, and a shake," Tai said.

I wonder what they will be serving, Izzy thought to himself. *Perhaps a big slab of meat, or some fish, and maybe some wa—*

"Water! Water!" T.K. yelled, interrupting Izzy's thoughts.

"Water?" Izzy said.

"Look, everybody!" T.K. said, running toward a big circular fountain. "A fresh water fountain! Hooray!"

One of the Yokos walked over to the fountain and puffed out his chest proudly. "All of the water here is piped in from a spring at Miharashi Mountain. It's the best water in the world!"

"Where's Mount Miharashi?" T.K. asked.

"UP THERE!" They all turned around and pointed to a huge cone-shaped mountain in the distance.

"Hey, that's a live volcano!" T.K. remarked.

"Yes, but the heat boils away all the germs," another Yokomon said.

It was almost as if the volcano was listening to their conversation, because the ground began to rumble.

"If I'm not mistaken, that noise precedes

an eruption," Izzy said.

Just then, the water fountain went dry. Instead of water pouring out, a huge column of flames streamed out through the fountain.

"*AAAAHHHH!*"

"What is happening?" Tai asked.

"The water evaporated," said one of the Yokomons. "That's okay because the lake is always *full* of water."

"I'll go check it out," Tai said bravely.

"Let's all go," Matt said.

The whole crew ran toward the lake to check the water. "Ooh, no!" they shouted as they reached the lakeshore. Because it was just a big empty hole.

"All right, let's not panic," Tai said. He grabbed a bucket and lowered it down into

a well right next to the lake. When he reeled it back up, there was only the charred end of the rope.

"Uh-oh!" Tai yelled, just as more flames came shooting up through the well shaft.

"Whoa!" Matt yelled. He stepped away from the well and thought for a second. "Hey, do you remember that flying gear we saw earlier?"

"It crashed," Mimi responded. "Right into a hillside."

"Great!" Sora said. "Of all the hillsides out there, the gear crashes right into Miharashi Mountain!"

"That's the place where the water comes from," Joe commented.

"That's right," one of the Yokomons said. "The water comes from a big lake on top of Mount Miharashi, so a gear crashing into the mountain *could* affect our water supply!"

Another Yokomon broke in. "We don't dare go up there. The mountain is guarded by a Fire Digimon called Meramon. He's hideously dangerous!"

Just then they all heard a loud wailing sound, as if someone were dying a slow, painful death. Tai used his binoculars to look up toward the mountain, where the wailing was coming from.

"There's Meramon," said Tai ". . . and he's coming this way!"

Imagine the body of a very strong, very tall man, except that the man's body was entirely covered by . . . *flames*! Well, that's what Meramon looked like, and he was sliding down the mountain toward them at top speed.

"He burns up everything he touches!" a Yokomon yelled.

"He *never* comes down off the mountain," another Yoko said. "This is *very strange* behavior for him."

"I'M BURNING! TOO HOT!" It was Meramon, still groaning and wailing from some sort of pain.

"Meramon is a Fire Digimon," one of the Yokos observed. "There's no reason he should be in pain from his own flames. That's his nature."

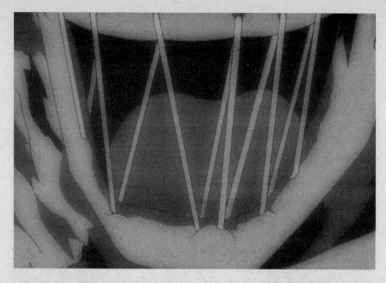

"This is weird," Tai said. "He's crying!"

"Sounds like he's out of his mind with pain!" Sora said.

"What do we do?" Tai asked.

"BURNNNING! BURRRNING! BURRRN-ING!"

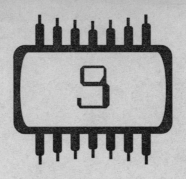

9

"Look, he's coming straight toward the village!" Sora exclaimed.

"We better do something quick!" a Yokomon said. "I've never seen him move so fast! He's already reached the foot of the mountain, and now he's heading for the forest!"

"Everybody freeze!" Sora barked. "Stay real still and maybe he won't see us."

"You're gonna need more than sunscreen to stop me!" Meramon shouted, his evil laughter filling the air.

"Burn! Burn! Burn!" Meramon's voice echoed through the valley. He was running through the forest toward them, igniting trees as he went. When he

finally emerged from the forest, it was obvious from his evil glare that their freeze tactic wouldn't work. Meramon was heading straight at them, and he was flaming mad.

"Unfreeze!" Tai yelled. "And ruuuunnn!"

They all turned and broke into a full sprint. Even the cute little Yokomons waddled away as fast as they could. They climbed down a cliff and ran into an abandoned ship that stuck out from the sand.

"Come on," Tai urged, standing in front of the ship to direct traffic. "Keep it moving!"

"All the way to the rear!" Sora commanded.

The Yokomons just kept coming in waves. They filed onto the ship like a bunch of panicked ants retreating into their anthill.

"Who's missing?" Sora asked Tai. She thought back to what she had heard earlier about "protecting her human friend." *Oh*

no, Sora thought, *Biyomon's in trouble.*

Sora looked up at the top of the cliff, where Biyomon was helping Yokos to escape. "Biyomon, save yourself!" Sora cried. "Now, while you still have time!"

"I can't leave here until all my friends are safe, Sora," Biyomon replied.

"All right," Sora replied. "I guess I'll just have to come up there after you, then!"

"Hurry up!" Tai said. "Sora—you'll never make it!"

Sora ran toward her and was approaching the bottom of the hill just as the last Yokos

were running toward the ship. The only one left at the top of the cliff . . . was Biyomon.

"Ahh, good," Biyomon said. "They're all safe now."

Sora looked up at Biyomon as she ran and noticed she was no longer alone. Behind her was a walking ball of flames with a bad attitude. "Biyo!" Sora called out. "Run, he's right behind you!"

"ROWRRR!!!"

Biyomon turned around and looked up at Meramon, who was just a few feet away. "Go away, Meramon! Leave us alone! We're not bothering you!"

But Meramon wasn't in the mood for a discussion. With one thunderous swat of his fiery arm, he sent Biyomon tumbling down the cliff, head over heels.

"Biyo! Biyo!" Sora chanted. "I'm coming, Biyo!"

Just as Biyomon fell to the ground, Sora took her last stride, jumped through the air, and caught her Digimon friend.

"Are you okay?" Sora asked breathlessly.

"Sure," Biyomon replied. "I hope I never do that again, though. It wasn't very much fun."

Sora chuckled. She picked Biyomon up and held her tight.

"Thank you for coming to rescue me," Biyomon said.

"Don't mention it," Sora said. "That's what friends are for."

"You can say that again, my friend," Biyomon agreed.

"*ARRRR!*"

"Uh-oh!" Biyomon cried. "We're still in great danger, Sora!"

"What?" Sora asked.

"You stay here—it's *my* turn to rescue *you* now!" Biyomon said. Biyo flew up to the top of the cliff and hovered in front of Meramon.

"You think you're really hot stuff, don't you?" Biyomon taunted. "Well, you're in big trouble now."

"SPIRAL TWISTER!"

Biyomon uncoiled her Spiral Twister attack, which landed right in Meramon's chest.

"Okay, Big Red! Take that!" Biyomon fired again and again. "And that! And that!"

"Haw! Haw! Haw!" Meramon cackled. Biyomon's Spiral Attack hadn't fazed him at all. "Is that the best you have to offer, weakling?"

"We gotta help her out!" Tai shouted. "He's too big to handle!"

"FIREBALL!" Meramon cried. He opened the palm of his hand, and a glowing ball of flames formed there. "Take *that*!" Meramon yelled, as he flung the fireball at Biyomon. It caught Biyomon right on the nose, and she sailed to the ground.

"Oh, no!" Sora called out. "She's hit!"

Tai looked at Sora and his face tightened. "Come on, everyone," he said. "We can beat this monster!"

All at once, Tentomon, Gabumon, and Patamon attacked Meramon with their most vicious assaults. But not only was Meramon uninjured, but he even seemed to gain power and grow after each blow.

"That made him bigger!" Matt said.

Meramon looked at the gang and groaned. "Why do I suffer so?" he said.

"I wish I knew what he was crying about," Tai said.

"Fire doesn't affect him," Izzy said. "So I'm guessing it's not heartburn."

"Maybe this monster just has growing pains," Matt said.

"Matt!" Joe shouted. "This is no time to joke!"

"Better get ready! Here I come!" Meramon shrieked, as he started down the cliff. He burst into another bout of loud, evil laughter.

Biyomon suddenly stood up from the spot where Meramon had knocked her to the ground. She could see that, if they didn't do something drastic, and *quick*, Meramon would turn into a pile of ashes.

"We're all in trouble now," Biyomon said. "Meramon *cannot* be allowed to win! My friends need my help now."

Immediately, a ray of white light shot from Sora's digivice and hit Biyomon right in the chest. The light became so powerful around Biyomon's body that she could no longer be seen. . . .

"Biyomon digivolve to . . . Birdramon!"

A shower of yellow and red lights sparked into the sky, then cleared away. And in the

space where Biyomon had been, a new creature that looked like an overfed orange hawk was in her place. *Birdramon* . . .

From the ship where they were all hiding, Sora, Tai, Agumon, and all the others heard a wild, shrieking battle cry and saw Birdramon wrestle Meramon. She tossed Meramon back over the cliff, then followed him with her talons ready for another attack.

"We'll be safe now!" Sora said hopefully. "Biyomon digivolved to rescue us!"

"KIYEEE!" Birdramon cried.

But Meramon wasn't done yet. He pulled himself off the ground and stood tall. "What's wrong, Birdramon . . . afraid of me? Let's fight! Here, have a ball!" He hurled another Fire Ball at Birdramon and struck her on the wing from behind. Birdramon let out a scream of anguish.

"Don't turn your back!" Sora called out.

Birdramon swooped toward Meramon at high speed. But Meramon was prepared. He hit Birdramon with a volley of Fire Balls. *POW! POW! POW!* They knocked Birdramon back so far that she could barely be seen in the distance.

But Birdramon was not so easily defeated.

She took a deep breath while hovering in the sky, and focused her powers. Then, with a mighty flap of her enormous, sparkling wings, Birdramon unleashed several golden heat rays. The attack, Meteor Wing, was considered one of the fiercest in DigiWorld.

Meramon cried out in pain, then shrunk to the ground with his head in his hands. Suddenly, a strange black disc flew out of Meramon's back and off into the sky. It was the Black Gear, which exploded into a cloud of dust in the sky.

"It was the gear!" Izzy exclaimed.

"It made him crazy!" Izzy said.

"I suppose if you had a big black gear stuck inside of you, you'd act a little crazy, too." Matt shook his head. "Poor guy."

"Yay!" T.K. cheered. "Biyomon did it!"

Birdramon transformed back into a little bird-like creature and hovered in midair. It was Biyomon!

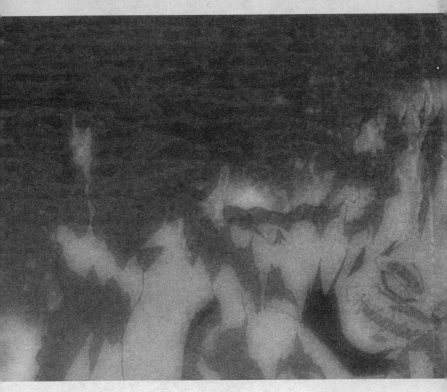

"Wow!" Sora said. "Every time I'm in danger, Biyomon comes to my rescue—she's the best friend I've got!"

"Are you all right?" Biyomon asked. She flew into Sora's arms and gave her a great big hug. "Oh, Sora!"

"Oh, Bee!" Sora said. "I was so worried about you! You're great. I can't even begin to tell you how proud I am of you."

"I wasn't the least bit afraid." Biyomon looked into her human friend's eyes. "All I could think about was saving you, because, Sora . . . well, you know . . ."

"Awww." Sora closed her eyes and smiled wide.

"I'll remember this day forever, Sora," Biyomon said.

Meramon was totally nice after the battle was over and the Black Gear was removed. He sat on the ground, surrounded by the kids, their Digimons, and dozens of Yokos. Imagine that!

"Meramon, why did you attack our village?" one of the Yokos asked.

Meramon rubbed his head. "I couldn't stop myself."

"That must have been awful for you." Yokomon paused. "If you couldn't control yourself, who was controlling you?"

"The last thing I remember is being hit by that gear," Meramon said.

"Well, we're just happy to see that you're back to nor-

mal," another Yokomon said. "I hope nothing like this ever happens again. You're needed to protect Mount Miharashi!"

Meramon nodded his head in agreement. Then he stood up and waved good-bye to everyone. He was heading back to Mount Miharashi.

"Good-bye, Meramon!" another Yokomon said. "May you always stay well! And please, try not to burn down our village anymore."

"Hey!" Biyomon said. She looked at Sora and smiled. "I just remembered you never got that dinner we promised you—You must be starving!"

"My stomach's ready for some action!" T.K. said.

"Yummy!"

"Let's eat!"

Cheers for a meal were heard all around. Many of them came from the Yokos, who seemed really excited to throw a dinner party for their newfound friends. They all scurried off into their huts and hurried back instantly with buckets full of food.

"What *is* this stuff?" Tai asked. He looked down into the yellow pellets that filled his food bucket. It really didn't look very appetizing.

Mimi shook her head at Tai. "Be polite and just eat it! A gracious guest never insults his host's cooking."

Biyomon smiled wide at her human friends. "Eat as much as you want," she declared. "We have more than enough for seconds."

"You know," Sora said. "That's exactly

what I was afraid you were going to say."

"Have you noticed how much we talk about food?" Matt asked. Then he scooped a pile of the food out with his hand and started stuffing his face.

"Actually, I'm not hungry," Sora said matter-of-factly.

"I'm skipping this one, too," Joe agreed. "I just don't like to eat on an empty stomach. . . . Besides, I don't know what this stuff is, but I'm sure I'm allergic to it."

The Yokos started laughing then at how

much of a worrywart Joe was. And the sound of their little high-pitched cackles were so funny that the whole crew joined in.

Amidst the laughter, Sora looked over at her friend Biyomon with pride. Biyo was chowing away at her Yoko food. She was so humble that you would never know that she had just been a fearless warrior in an epic battle.

One thing is for certain, Sora thought to herself, *for being so little, Biyomon sure has a huge heart. . . .*